The Great Necklace Hunt

Roman stories linking in with the
National Curriculum Key Stage 2

First published in 1995 by Watts Books
96 Leonard Street, London EC2A 4RH

Franklin Watts Australia
14 Mars Road
Lane Cove
NSW 2066

Series editor: Paula Borton
Consultant: Joan Blyth
Designer: Kirstie Billingham

A CIP catalogue record for this book
is available from the British Library.

ISBN 0 7496 2221 0

Dewey Classification 942.01

Printed in Great Britain

F
GOW

The Great Necklace Hunt

by
Mick Gowar

Illustrations by Martin Remphry

Watts Books
London • New York • Sydney

Helena Julia Marcus Gaius

Lucius Druscilla Livia

1

Showing Off

Helena pulled aside the thick woollen curtain that hung in the doorway and slipped into her mother's bedroom.

"This'll show her," muttered Helena. "This'll show that boastful Livia!"

She peered round the room. The

shutters were closed to keep out the summer heat. The room was cool and dark.

Helena let her eyes get used to the gloom. In front of her was the bed with its thick, brightly coloured quilt. Beside the bed was a soft, thick mat, also brightly coloured. To one side of the bed was a stiff, straight-backed wicker chair. And against the wall, at the other side of the bed, was what Helena was looking for - the heavy wooden chest where her mother kept all her clothes and jewellery.

Helena began to creep across the room. There was a loud CLANG! Pain shot through her right foot. She bit her lip to stop herself screaming out, and looked down to

see what had done the damage. She'd kicked a large, empty chamber pot.

Helen sat down and rubbed her toes through her open sandal. She couldn't stop a tear rolling down her cheek.

"It's all Livia's fault," she said to herself.

Ever since Helena, her mother and her brother had come to stay with Uncle Lucius and his family, Helena's cousin Livia had hardly stopped boasting long enough to draw breath. She boasted about how her father, who was a magistrate and tax collector, earned pots and pots more money than Helena's father did in the army. Livia had a pitying look that she turned on Helena when she said things like, "Our house in Verulamium must seem *so* luxurious after what you're used to..." and, "It must seem *so* strange to you to be living in a house with *so* many slaves..." It made Helena grind her teeth in rage.

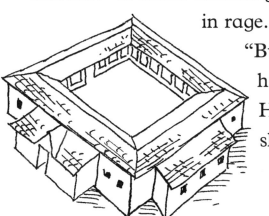

"But I'll show her," muttered Helena. "I'll show her!"

She clambered to her feet and crept over to the large wooden chest. She lifted the lid - CRASH! It swung back and hit the wall.

Helena stood absolutely still. The crash was so loud she was sure that any minute she'd hear the sound of running footsteps, and voices shouting, "What's the matter?" "*What* was that terrible noise?" "Has the roof collapsed?" She waited...and waited...and waited. Nothing.

Helena let out a sigh of relief. She knelt down in front of the chest, and carefully

 folded back the damask cloth. There was her mother's special box.

Helena lifted it out of the chest. It was a round box made of ivory. Helena's hands traced the carved figures of running cherubs that decorated the box. Then, curling her fingers round the carved ivory pine cone, she lifted the round lid and placed it carefully on the floor beside her.

Helena scrabbled among the earrings and brooches, and lifted out a string of polished jet beads. Even in the half-light of the shuttered bedroom the black beads gleamed.

"This'll make Livia jealous," she said to herself. "Really, *really* jealous!" Helena slipped the necklace over her head.

She tiptoed out of the room. Livia was waiting in the corridor.

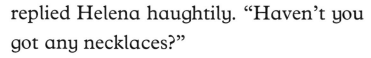

"Is that really yours?" asked Livia suspiciously.

"Of course," replied Helena haughtily. "Haven't you got any necklaces?"

"Piles and piles," replied Livia. "Boxes and boxes of them."

"Well, I've never seen you wearing any," sneered Helena.

"Erm..." For once Livia seemed lost for words. "It's just..." there was another pause, "they're all gold, and they're much too valuable to wear," she said quickly.

"I don't believe you," snapped Helena.

Livia ignored her. "Let me look at them," she demanded, stretching out her hand to touch the shiny black beads around Helena's neck.

"No!" said Helena, pulling away.

"Yes!" insisted Livia. "This is my house, and you're just a guest. You have to do what I say!" She lunged forward and grabbed the necklace.

"NO!" yelled Helena, trying to pull herself free.

For a couple of seconds they tugged back and forth, then Helena staggered back as the string

snapped and the beads rattled and
bounced across the shining tiles of the
mosaic floor.

"Oh, no!" gasped Helena. "What will
my mother say? And my father? He'll be
furious! He gave her the necklace when
they first —"

"Ah ha!" crowed Livia triumphantly.
"So they weren't yours after all? I knew it!"

Helena was already on her hands and

knees. "Help me pick up the beads - quickly, before anyone sees us!"

"Why should I help you?" asked Livia. "You lied to me."

"It was all your fault the necklace broke," snapped Helena. "You grabbed it."

The two girls scrabbled across the tiled floor frantically gathering black beads.

"Is that all of them?" asked Livia, after a few minutes.

"I think so," replied Helena uncertainly.

"Miss Livia! Miss Helena! Where are you?" The loud voice of Marcia, Livia's nurse, echoed along the corridors of the large house.

"MISS LIVIA! MISS HELENA!" Marcia's voice was shrill with worry.

Helena held up her handful of beads. "What can we do?" she asked. "We've got to get rid of them before Marcia sees them."

"Here -" Livia pointed to a big, blue-glazed vase that was standing against the wall. "We can fetch them later," she whispered.

Marcia lumbered along the corridor.

"There you are!" she panted.

She was red in the face. Damp strands of hair were stuck to her forehead. "I've been looking for you everywhere!"

The two girls clambered to their feet. Marcia noticed their flushed faces.

"What have you been doing?" she asked.

"Errr...nothing, Marcia," replied Livia lightly.

"Well, hurry up with you," scolded Marcia. "It's almost the end of the ninth hour,

and you should be getting ready for supper. And there's a special treat for you, Miss Helena."

"What's that, Marcia?" asked Helena.

"Well, I shouldn't really tell you, because it's supposed to be a secret..." Marcia hesitated. She had never been able to keep a secret. "But as you've asked me so nicely, I'll tell you. Your father's on his way back from Londinium. He'll be with us tonight!"

2

A Small Supper

The fading light made the bright pictures of harvest scenes and wine-making that covered the walls of the dining room look misty and dim.

"It's time for the slaves to light the lamps," thought Helena. "Almost time for bed."

As she waited for the main course to
be cleared away, Helena looked round the
big square room again. There were three
large couches, covered with mattresses,
arranged around a low, square marble
table. On the middle couch, Helena's
father and Uncle Lucius lounged and

chatted. On the left hand couch lay Livia's
mother and Aunt Druscilla. On the right,
all on his own, was Helena's brother,
Gaius. Helena and Livia were too young
to eat from couches and sat on stools near
their mothers. Everyone seemed to be
happy and enjoying the meal and the

company - everyone except Helena.

Helena gazed down at the uneaten chicken leg lying on her cloth napkin and sighed.

"Helena?"

No answer.

"Helena!"

"Oh, sorry - yes, Mother?"

Julia looked worried. "You've hardly eaten a thing and chicken has always been your favourite. Is something the matter, child? Do you feel unwell? Have you got a pain?"

Helena shook her head.

Helena's aunt Druscilla shook her head and clucked like a nosy hen.

"My friend Lenia's sister-in-law's youngest was like that," she said in a whisper that could be heard in every corner of the room. "Wouldn't eat, wouldn't speak. Then three days later —" She paused dramatically. Her thickly painted eyebrows shot up and she shook her head sadly and clucked again.

Before Aunt Druscilla could say any more the slaves came in to remove the discarded bones and the few shreds of lettuce left on the serving dishes. Then they came back with jugs of perfumed water and towels to wash the diners' greasy hands.

For dessert Helena chose a small brown apple, which she fiddled with but didn't eat.

"Only a few more minutes," she thought, "and I can go to bed. Then it won't be long till morning and I can get the beads back. And then..." Helena didn't know what she was going to do. She knew she would have to mend the necklace, but she didn't know how. Maybe Livia would know. Even if she was a snob, Livia always had good ideas about how to get out of trouble.

When the last of the meal had been cleared away, Aunt Druscilla, after a discreet belch, turned on her side to face Helena's father.

"Marcus," she said, "you haven't told us what happened on your trip to Londinium. Is it true that you saw the governor himself?"

Marcus's tanned face went red.

"Uh-oh!" thought Helena. "He's getting cross!" Marcus had a quick temper.

He coughed, and scratched the back of his neck - a sure sign that he felt awkward about something.

"That's not entirely true, Druscilla. But I have got some exciting news to tell you all," he looked round at the semi-

circle of eager faces, "*tomorrow*. Lucius
has invited my old friend and patron,
Aulus Platorious to dinner tomorrow night.
I will tell you all then."

Aunt Druscilla opened her mouth. She
looked annoyed. Helena guessed that she
was about to protest about being given so
little time to prepare a meal for such an
important guest. But Uncle Lucius shot
her a stern warning glance. She shut her
mouth again smartly.

"Julia, my dear," said Marcus. As a special favour to me will you wear your jet bead necklace - you know, the one I bought you when we first met?"

Helena's mother smiled. "Why, of course my dear," she replied. Then she noticed Helena's face which had turned a sickly greyish white colour.

"Helena! What *is* the matter?"

Helena stood up.

"I...I...I...feel sick!" she blurted out, and ran from the room as fast as she could.

3

Mysteries

Lucius was up at dawn next morning to supervise the cleaning of the house.

"Come on, lad!" bellowed Lucius. "Get those cobwebs down."

The skinny slave at the top of the ladder peered upwards.

"Cobwebs, master?"

"There, boy - *there!*" Lucius pointed.

The slave made vague sweeping-type movements with a wooden handled brush, but the cobweb did not budge.

Lucius turned to Marcus who was standing beside him. "You can't get decent household slaves in Britain these days."

Marcus nodded. "It's the same in the

army - weedy, knock-kneed mummy's boys who haven't got the strength to lift a javelin, let alone throw it with enough force to —"

"Look out!" yelled Lucius suddenly.

Marcus looked up and saw the slave teetering and swaying on the top of the ladder. He dropped the brush and grabbed the top of the ladder. The brush hit the blue vase underneath with a great clatter.

"You clumsy fool!" shouted Lucius picking up the vase to examine it. "You could have —"

Lucius stopped in mid-sentence.

Something wasn't right. He shook the
vase. It rattled.

"If you've broken it..." he growled.

He plunged his right hand into the vase.

"What's this?" He held out his hand to
Marcus. "Jet beads, that's strange. Neither
Druscilla or Livia have any jewellery like
this, I'm sure."

"Let me see," said Marcus. There was
something familiar
about the beads.

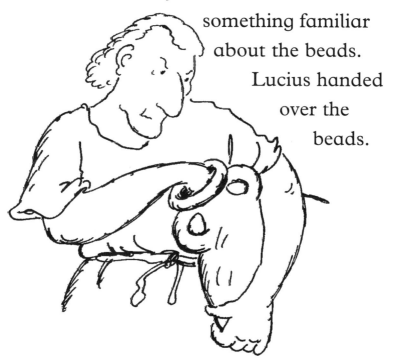

Lucius handed
over the
beads.

Marcus began to
arrange them on
the palm of his
broad,
muscular
hand.

"Four
round...then three oval, then...
four round." He looked at Lucius.

"I don't believe it, but I swear these are
the beads from Julia's necklace. But how
could they have got into the vase?"

Lucius shrugged. "Maybe the necklace
broke, and she was too frightened to tell
you —"

"Frightened of *me*?" Marcus
interrupted angrily. "Why should she be
frightened of me?"

"You can be short-tempered at times.

Anyway, what matters is that you've got
them now," Lucius continued, "you could
have them re-strung for her as a surprise.
Then you could present them to her at
dinner, tonight."

"But how can I get them restrung?"
asked Marcus.

"There's an excellent jeweller in the
Forum," Lucius replied. "I've bought a

couple of things from him for Druscilla.
Very good work, and not too expensive. As
soon as we've finished here, we can go and
see him."

"They're not here!" shrieked Helena.

"They must be," said Livia. "Look
again."

"They're not!" insisted Helena. She
turned the large blue
vase upside down
and shook it.
Nothing fell out.

"What are we
going to do?" asked
Livia.

Helena's only
answer was to
burst into tears.

Marcia came bustling up the corridor.
"Miss Livia! Miss Helena!" she called.
She stopped when she saw
Helena's face.

"Miss Helena!
What's wrong? Are
you unwell?
Whatever is

the matter?" She seemed more upset than the two girls. "Oh dear, oh dear, oh dear! Where does it hurt, Miss Helena? We'll have to fetch the doctor. And cancel the dinner for tonight. Where is the pain, Miss Helena? In your stomach?"

"It's not that," Livia interrupted. "She's not ill, it's just that...well, errr...."

"What's the matter?" asked Marcia again. She put a plump, motherly arm round Helena's shoulders. Come on, child. You can tell me."

Helena controlled her sobs, and the two girls explained what had happened. As they talked, Marcia's eyes grew wider and wider. "Oh dear, oh dear, oh dear..." she kept repeating.

"You two have been very naughty indeed!" she said when the two children

had finished their story.

"But what are we going to *do*?" asked Livia.

Marcia thought for a minute. "There's one person I know who might be able to help - a jeweller in the Forum. He's made some lovely things for the mistress. We'll go and see him this morning. Do you have any money, Miss Helena?"

"A little," replied Helena with a sniff. "Why?"

"To pay for the necklace," replied Marcia. "But think yourself lucky that you're getting no worse punishment!" And she patted her round bottom and looked sternly at the two girls.

"I can't understand it," said Julia, shaking her head. "I was sure that I'd brought it with me, but I've searched my box and the chest in my bedroom and there's no sign of the necklace anywhere."

"When did you last wear it?" asked Druscilla.

"Oh, ages ago," replied Julia. "To tell the truth, I don't even like it. It wasn't very expensive and it's not very pretty.

But Marcus gave it to me years ago, and he'll be *furious* when he finds out I've lost it."

"Well, then - don't tell him," said Druscilla with a sly smile. "Simply buy a new one and he'll never know!"

"But where....how?"

"There's a wonderful little man who sells jewellery in the Forum. I bought some gorgeous earrings from him when Lucius was away on a trip to Camulodunum. I could send one of the slaves —"

"No, no!" Julia shook her head. "I'll have to go myself. It'll have to be an exact copy of the necklace or Marcus will notice. Besides," she blushed, "I don't want *anyone* to know. May I use your litter?"

"Of course," replied Druscilla sweetly.

"Thank you," said Julia with a sigh.

"I'd better go straight away if I'm to have the necklace by tonight. And remember, Druscilla, not a word to anyone."

Druscilla looked shocked. "As if I would! You can trust me, Julia! You can trust *me!*"

4

A Bumpy Ride

"Being carried by litter maybe dignified,"
thought Julia as she was joggled through
the gateway that led into the Forum, "but
it is *very* uncomfortable. *Ouch!*" she
exclaimed as the litter jerked to a
temporary halt. It didn't help when one of

the slaves carrying the poles was many
inches shorter than the other three.

Julia peered out through the curtains
that surrounded the couch she was lying
on. The Forum was crowded today.
Around the pillared walkways, groups of
people were chatting in the shade.

A procession was making its way across
the open square towards the temple of
Jupiter, leading a white bull that would be
the sacrifice. Two dancers were
entertaining a crowd on one side of the
square, and eager shoppers clustered
around the market stalls.

Julia pulled the curtain further back so she could get a better view. "The first stall on the left, facing the Basilica," she murmured to herself, remembering the directions Druscilla had given her.

"Stop here!" she called out to the litter bearers. "Let me down —"

Then she saw two familiar figures standing by the very stall she was going to. "Marcus!" she gasped. "And Lucius!

Quickly!" she commanded the litter slaves. "We can't stop now! Take me - um - all the way round the Forum and then back here."

She could hear the weary groans and sighs as the slaves lifted the litter back onto their shoulders. Julia could tell the slaves weren't happy.

"*Ouch!*" There was a huge jolt as the litter resumed its lopsided progress between the crowds. Julia rubbed her bruised bottom. No, the slaves weren't happy at all.

"You see, I told you he'd be able to do it," said Lucius, as the two men turned away from the jeweller's stall and began to push their way through the crowds.

"A bit expensive, though," said Marcus grumpily, "for a bit of thread." He jiggled the re-strung necklace in his hand.

Lucius grinned. "But think how delighted Julia will be."

Marcus shrugged. "I hope so," he said.

Behind them, Owain, the jeweller, grinned broadly as he slipped the coins into his purse. "More money than sense," he muttered to himself. "The perfect customers!"

He was just arranging some necklaces on the stall, when he was interrupted by two little girls and a plump woman.

"Are you Owain, the jeweller?" asked the plump woman.

"At your service," replied Owain.

"I believe you have made some jewellery for my mistress, the Lady Druscilla, wife of Lucius the magistrate."

"Ah, yes," said Owain, grinning broadly. "It's always a pleasure to do work for his lordship's household. What would you like me to do?"

"*Ouch!*"

The litter came to a halt with another bump. Julia could hear the slaves panting and gasping for breath. It was a very hot day to jog round the Forum carrying a heavy litter. But Lucius and

Marcus *must* be gone by now.

Julia parted the curtains and looked out.

"Oh, gods!" she gasped. "Marcia, Helena and Livia. *Keep going!*" she shouted to the slaves.

There was a long pause.

"Quickly!" called Julia. "Once more round the Forum, and back here."

There were loud groans, and rather loud mutterings of "Oh, no," and, "What's she trying to *do* to us?" from the litter bearers.

"Do as you are told!" Julia said in her most commanding voice. "Round the Forum and back here!"

The litter gave another dramatic lurch as the slaves lumbered off on another exhausting lap of the Forum.

"*Owwww!*"

5

Surprises

Julia walked into the dining room a little stiffly. Despite the bath, the large purple bruises ached. But it had been worth it! She beamed at her husband who was reclining on the couch facing her. She bowed her head to Aulus Platorious,

who was sitting in the place of honour to the right of her brother-in-law Lucius.

"I apologise for being late, but I had to look for something rather special," she explained, blushing. She lifted her hand to her throat and stroked the black bead necklace she was wearing. Owain the jeweller had made it in less than an hour. "He was as good a craftsman as Druscilla had said," thought Julia, "but why did he grin all the time in that horrid way?"

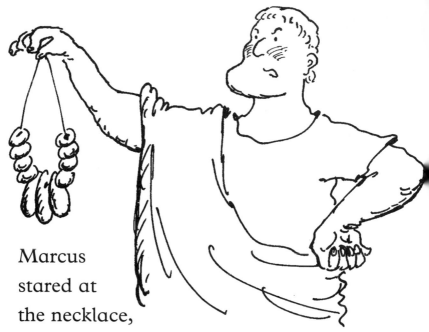

Marcus
stared at
the necklace,
then down at his clenched fist. He looked
dumbfounded. Then he stood up and held
out his hand. "But I have your necklace,
here!"

"Ooooooh!" wailed Helena.

Everyone in the room turned to stare
at her.

"B-b-b-but, Mother," she stammered.

"I've got your necklace, too!" And she held out a third necklace.

There was complete silence in the room. Then Marcus, his face red with anger, bellowed, "What is going on? *This* is your necklace!"

"Calm down, Marcus," hissed Lucius. "Don't forget our guest."

Lucius nodded in the direction of Aulus Platorious. Nobody moved. Nobody breathed.

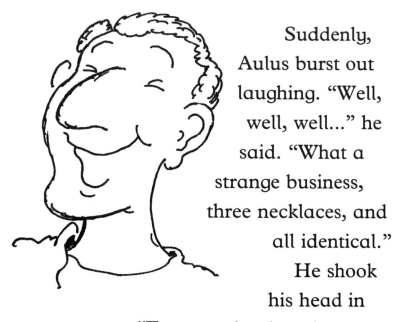

Suddenly, Aulus burst out laughing. "Well, well, well..." he said. "What a strange business, three necklaces, and all identical." He shook his head in amusement. "Fortunately, there is a simple solution. If you will allow me....." He stood up. "The lady Julia," he bowed, "has her necklace." He took the necklace from Marcus and walked over to the couch where Druscilla was lying. "Which leaves one for our lovely hostess," he presented the necklace to Druscilla. "And one —" he walked over to where Helena was standing, "for the Lady Helena to keep for when she is old enough to wear it. Is that a fair solution?"

There was a moment's silence, then Lucius clapped his hands.

"Bravo!" he cried. "Excellent! And Marcus agrees with me - *don't you Marcus?*"

Marcus still looked red-faced, but managed to force a smile.

"Which reminds me," continued
Lucius. "You've got some exciting news for
us, haven't you Marcus?"

"Errm, yes," Marcus cleared his
throat. "As you all know, Aulus Platorious
is the Imperial Legate. He has done me
the honour to ask me to serve as Camp
Prefect for the Sixth Legion, who are
helping to
complete
the

building of the Great North Wall. I take
up my command next week, and Gaius,
you can accompany me."

Gaius's face shone with delight.

"And Julia and Helena, you can join
us soon. There are comfortable quarters in
the main fort, so we can all be together!"

Julia tried her best to keep smiling.
"The Great North Wall?" she thought.
"The Great North Freezing Wall!"

"Now isn't that wonderful news?"
beamed Lucius.
"Congratulations!"

Roman Town Life

In this story, Helena and her family are made up
characters, but in a lot of ways they were like
many real Roman families who lived at that time.

Roman houses

Houses for well-off people like Helena's uncle
would be quite large and divided up into rooms like
ours are today. Bedrooms would not have much
furniture in them, but places like the dining room
would have pictures painted on the walls in the
same way as we would have wallpaper. In towns in
Italy, houses would have wooden shutters on the
windows, but in Britain where it was cold and wet
windows would have thick glass.

Roman clothes and jewellery

Romans wore a tunic. Rich women might wear a long dress over the top, called a *stola,* Men wore togas. They were usually worn on special occasions such as banquets and special dinners. Many people disliked wearing them as they were heavy and awkward.

Romans loved jewellery of all kinds, and as most of their clothes were made from large uncut pieces of material, they also wore brooches and special pins to fasten their garments together.

Roman towns

At the centre of each town was the Forum. It was the town square as well as the market place. It was a good place for people to meet. At one end of the Forum was the basilica. Inside the basilica were magistrates' courts, tax offices and the meeting place for the town council.

Roman food

Romans ate *lentculum* - breakfast, *prandium* - lunch and *cena* - *dinner*.

For *lentculum* they would have bread and a cup of wine mixed with water. *Prandium* would probably be bread or leftovers. Their main meal was *cena* which might consist of many courses. We would think some of the food they ate was very strange. Stuffed dormice was thought to be a real treat. Maybe dormice were served at dinner in honour of Aulus Platorius!